A Toy Train Under the Christmas Tree

Story by Allen C. Harper

THE
DESTINY TOY COMPANY
MODEL NO. 9 TRAIN

Illustrated by Agnes I. Klimek

Aleo Publications

DUNDEE, ILLINOIS

Story by Allen C. Harper
Cover design and illustrations by Agnes I. Klimek

Book design and format by Philip A. Aleo

Editor: Elizabeth A. Green

Published by Aleo Publications, division of P.F.C. Supply Co. Inc.
P.O. Box 1085, Dundee, IL 60118
www.aleopublications.com

Printed in the United States of America

Printed by Carlith LLC, Carpentersville, IL.

ISBN: 978-0-9856081-4-9

Library of Congress Control Number: 2013944651

Dedicated to Grandma Flora,
Grandma Mellie Mae,
Grandma Marion
and to all grandmothers
who create some of the best memories
of our lives.

Allen C. Harper

It was a week before Christmas. Eight-year-old Jimmy sat on his grandma's kitchen floor looking at her old catalogs. Grandma said when she was a girl they used the books to shop for things.

"We didn't have computers, or the Internet," Grandma told Jimmy. "Most people shopped in stores. If they lived far from town like we did, they ordered what they needed from catalogs like the one you're reading."

As he turned the pages, Jimmy saw toys and clothes, even things like vacuum cleaners and tools. It wasn't that different from looking for things on the computer.

"Here is a special Christmas catalog," Grandma said, pointing to another book. "I used to cut out pictures of my favorite toys and clothes and paste them in a scrapbook. It was fun to look at the pictures and dream about them."

Jimmy loved visiting his grandma. She always told him great stories and did fun things with him.

Grandma had an idea. Jimmy could make a scrapbook of his own. He might like pretending to be a boy back in the old days. She put some pieces of paper, a roll of tape, and a pair of round-end scissors on the dining room table, then placed the catalog beside them.

"Let's play a game. You can cut out pictures of the toys you like, just the way I used to do. Then we can make a scrapbook of your favorites," she said.

Jimmy thought that was a great idea. He sat down at the table, and opened the catalog to the first page. There were pages and pages of toys.

"It's only pretend, but it never hurts to dream," Grandma said.

Jimmy turned the pages slowly. These weren't the kind of toys he was used to. He didn't see any action figures, or electronic games. The scissors just sat on the table. Where were the toys he could dream about?

Grandma went to the kitchen to make their lunch. When it was ready, she went back to get Jimmy. He sat at the table quietly, with the catalog closed in front of him.

"I thought you would have a big pile of pictures by now," Grandma said.

"Toys are really different now, Grandma," Jimmy said with a smile. "I did find one that I like, a lot."

He handed her a single picture with jagged edges.

THE DESTINY TOY COMPANY MODEL NO. 9 TRAIN

C Whistles and puffs smoke!

THE DESTINY TOY COMPANY

9

The most realistic toy train ever made. Children will think it is magical.

Grandma read the description out loud, "The Destiny Toy Company Model No. 9 Train. The most realistic toy train ever made. Children will think it is magical."

Jimmy's eyes opened wide. "A magical train! I could dream about asking Santa to bring me that train for Christmas."

He stopped and looked at Grandma. She was very quiet, and had a far-away look in her eyes. "Grandma, did Santa bring you the things you wished for when you were a girl?"

"Not always," she said. "When I was your age, I would get up Christmas morning, just certain Santa had left what I wanted under the tree. Sometimes he did, but other times I would be so sad when I didn't find what I had wished for."

That didn't seem fair. Jimmy knew Santa couldn't bring everything children asked for. When he got his bike last year, he knew it was very special and would be his only present. But even if Grandma was extra good when she was a girl, Santa didn't always bring her what she wished and dreamed about.

9

"When I was disappointed, my mom and dad reminded me
 that Christmas celebrates the birth of the baby Jesus,"
Grandma said kindly. "They said he gave all of us the best
gift ever and never asked for anything but love!"

She knew it was difficult for Jimmy
to understand. It was hard for her
when she was a girl, too.

Grandma smiled. She had an idea
how she could help Jimmy learn
the true meaning of Christmas.

"Tomorrow we are going to do
some giving," she said.

"What do you mean?"
Jimmy asked with a funny look.

"Wait and see," she said.

The next morning Jimmy awoke clutching the picture of The Destiny Toy Company Model No. 9 Train.

He could see that Grandma had some special plans. Beside his usual oatmeal and glass of milk were a pencil and paper. On the counter were a rolling pin, cookie cutters, and baking pans.

"We're going to make cookies, aren't we Grandma?"

"Absolutely," said Grandma, "but not for us."

Jimmy was startled. "What are you going to do with all the cookies?"

13

neighbor? my teacher, Mail man,
a cousin? bus driver? my friend?

Grandma looked at him patiently and said, "We are going
to celebrate Christmas."

She picked up the pencil and paper and handed them to Jimmy.

"I want you to make a list of people you would never give a gift to, people
you have seen but never met, and perhaps some you are even afraid of.
You are going to give each of them a bag of Christmas cookies."

Jimmy was confused. "How can I include somebody I don't
even know?" he asked. He sat quietly for a few minutes, then looked
up with a big smile.

"If I give all these cookies away, do you think Santa will bring me
The Destiny Toy Company Model No. 9 Train?"

"Maybe, and maybe not," Grandma answered. "It's sort of like the name
on the train. It has to be your destiny. If it's meant to be, it will be.
Now eat your breakfast and start making your list. When you're done,
we'll bake cookies."

Jimmy stared at his picture of The Destiny Toy Company Model No. 9
Train as he tried to think of ideas for his list. One by one, he wrote
descriptions of people he had seen around town. Then he folded the paper
and put it in his pocket.

"I'm ready to make the cookies," he said.

He and his grandma had fun smooshing the butter, then mixing in the flour and sugar, along with what Grandma called her secret ingredients. They rolled out the cookie dough, then used cookie cutters to make Christmas trees, stars, reindeer, Santas, and snowmen.

They baked the cookies, decorated them with frosting and sprinkles and put them into plastic bags.

"You were a very good helper, Jimmy," Grandma said. "Tomorrow we'll deliver a bag of cookies to each person on your list."

The next day Grandma and Jimmy headed out to deliver the cookies. Before they left, she handed Jimmy some crisp dollar bills.

"You might need these, too" she said.
"Where should we go first?"

"Well, I remembered that man who washes your windshield when you stop at the traffic light. Maybe he would like some cookies," Jimmy said.

"That's a good idea, Jimmy. He's poor and may not have a home," Grandma said with a smile.

The man was standing on the street corner as Grandma pulled up to the stop light. Jimmy had always felt a little afraid of him because his clothes were old and dirty. But with his grandma there, he wasn't frightened.

Jimmy rolled down his window and handed the man a bag of Christmas tree cookies and two dollar bills.

The man looked shocked, but with a toothless smile said, "God Bless you, lad, and Merry Christmas to you."

WHOO-OOO-oooo!

As Grandma drove away, Jimmy heard a train whistle just like he imagined the Destiny Toy Company Model No. 9 Train would have.

"Grandma, did you hear that?" Jimmy said.

"Hear what, dear?" Grandma replied.

Before Jimmy could answer, she said, "Where are we going next?"

"The mall," Jimmy said sheepishly. "I thought maybe the man who wears the Santa hat and rings the bell would like some cookies too."

"That's a great idea," Grandma said. "He is a volunteer for the Salvation Army, and they help lots of people with the money they collect."

Jimmy felt excited as he walked up to the man, not scared or embarrassed like he usually did. He dropped a dollar bill in the shiny red bucket, then handed the man a bag of Santa cookies.

The man was caught off guard, but quickly recovered with a hearty "Ho, Ho, Ho" and said to Jimmy, "God Bless you, young man."

WH00-000-0000!

As he turned to get back into Grandma's car, Jimmy thought he saw The Destiny Toy Company Model No. 9 Train scoot behind a row of shopping carts. Then he heard the train whistle again.

WH00-000-0000!

"Grandma, did you see that?" Jimmy asked. Looking closer, he saw nothing was there.

"See what?" Grandma said as she started the car. "Next stop?"

"The park where I like to play. I've seen a man in a wheelchair there," Jimmy said. "I bet he would like some of our cookies."

As they walked into the park, Jimmy spotted the man wearing a baseball cap that read "Vietnam, US Army Special Forces." Grandma told Jimmy he was a war veteran who might have been hurt defending our country.

Jimmy ran up to the man and gave him a bag of star-shaped Christmas cookies. Shyly, he thanked him for being in the Army, then added, "Merry Christmas, sir."

At first, the veteran said nothing. Then with a tear in his eye, the man said, "Bless you child, this is the nicest thing anyone has done for me in years."

Jimmy nodded and this time walked very slowly back to the car.

WHOO-OOO-oooo!

As he started to open the car door he heard a train whistle and saw The Destiny Toy Company Model No. 9 Train go under some bushes.

When he looked around the bushes, nothing was there.

Jimmy got back into the car and Grandma asked him, "What were you doing over there?"

"Oh, nothing. I was just looking around," Jimmy said with a smile. "Let's go to my school next. There are some guys who play basketball there all the time. I thought they might like some cookies too."

25

At the school, Jimmy nervously walked up to the boys.

"My grandma wanted me to share these Christmas cookies with people I don't know," he said. "I've seen you around school, and thought it would be nice to meet you."

The tallest of the boys tucked the ball under his arm and walked over to where Jimmy stood. He stared for a few moments, then said, "Hey man, those look good!" Soon the other players came over and helped themselves to the cookies.

Jimmy said, "My grandma and I made them together."

The first boy replied, "You tell her she makes good snowman cookies. Thanks, and have a Merry Christmas."

26

WHOO-OOO-oooo!

The boy turned his head suddenly. "What was that?" he said. "I thought I heard a train whistle."

Jimmy laughed to himself and said he had to go. All the boys agreed to see each other at school after the Christmas holiday.

"One more stop," Grandma said. "Where to?"

"Can we go to the hospital?" Jimmy said. "When I broke my arm last summer, Mom took me there. It really hurt and I cried an awful lot. The nurses and the doctor were very nice to me. I think some reindeer cookies will make them happy."

Jimmy shook off all his bad memories of that day and walked right into the emergency room.

He handed the bag of Christmas cookies to the woman at the reception desk and told her why he was there. The woman smiled, "I remember you. How's that arm now?"

"Much better," Jimmy said. "Thanks."

The woman called to the nurses, "Look, everyone. This boy brought us cookies."

Then she turned to Jimmy. "You have given us a gift. Not just cookies, but the love that Christmas is all about," she said. "I hope you have a wonderful, blessed Christmas!"

Jimmy was thinking this was the best stop of all as he looked down the hallway.

WHOO-OOO-oooo ! Was that a toy train going into a room?

Jimmy and Grandma went back to her car.

"Well Jimmy, you did a great job today. You gave others the gift of Christmas and made people happy," she said. "Now it's time to go home."

"Not yet, Grandma. Can we make another stop?" Jimmy said.

"But why? We already gave away all our cookies," she said with surprise.

"I need to drop off a special gift. It's important to me," Jimmy said.

"Okay," his Grandma said. "Where do you want me to drive?"

Jimmy blurted out, "Can you take me over to the little church down the street from our house? Please?"

The church was beautiful, especially at Christmas time with its life size nativity scene on the lawn. There were statues of Joseph, Mary, the three Wise Men with their gifts, and all sorts of animals. Right in the very middle was a manger, and in it lay the baby Jesus.

Jimmy got out of the car and walked over to the manger.

Grandma watched her grandson reach into his pocket and pull out a carefully folded piece of paper. It was the page from her Christmas catalog, his picture of The Destiny Toy Company Model No. 9 Train.

Jimmy carefully placed the paper under the blanket covering the baby Jesus, then slowly walked back to the car. Grandma and Jimmy both sat silently for a few moments. Finally she said, "You gave Jesus the train."

Jimmy answered simply, "Jesus gave us the best gift of all and even though he didn't ask for anything in return, I think he would like The Destiny Toy Company Model No. 9 Train."

And, so the day of Christmas cookies and "giving" ended. It was a good day!

The next week, Jimmy was back home with his mom and dad.

On Christmas morning, Jimmy woke up early. It was hard to wait until his mom and dad got up. He could hear the old grandfather clock in the living room going tick tock, tick tock.

"Merry Christmas," his mom finally called from the hall. "Let's go see what Santa has left under the tree."

There were several boxes, all brightly wrapped and tied with colorful ribbons. Their stockings hung by the fireplace, bulging with oranges and candy canes.

Jimmy was thrilled with his new toys, a basketball, some of his favorite books, and a new sweater. But he was a tiny bit sad when he realized there was no Destiny Toy Company Model No. 9 Train under the tree.

Jimmy and his parents had finished opening their gifts when suddenly there was a noise at the door.

BUMP! BUMP! BUMP!

Jimmy's mom looked out the window.
There was no one there.

A short time later they heard the noise again.

BUMP! BUMP! BUMP!

This time Dad got up and looked out the window.
There was no one there.

A few minutes later, Jimmy heard something at the front door.

BUMP! BUMP! BUMP!

They all went to see what was making the noise. No one was there.

WHOO-OOO-oooo!

They looked down.

A beautiful toy train ran right past their feet and into the living room. Jimmy shrieked with joy and exclaimed, "It's The Destiny Toy Company Model No. 9 Train!"

WH00-000-0000!

The little train headed straight for the Christmas tree. It ran in circles around and around under the tree.

Then just as quickly, the train sped past them and out the front door.

The train had not come to stay.

Jimmy wasn't sad to see it go. The train had helped him learn the importance of giving to others. It let him know he could overcome his fears and reach out to help people, even the ones he didn't know.

He already had the best Christmas present of all: the gift of Jesus.
That was the true Christmas spirit.

Where the train was going, no one knew.

Somewhere, there was another boy or girl who could learn from
The Destiny Toy Company Model No. 9 Train.

It was just like Grandma said. What was meant to be, was meant to be.

It was destiny.

Grandma's Famous Sugar Cookies
Bake at 375 Degrees F.

1-1/2 cups powdered sugar
1 cup butter softened
1 egg
2 teaspoons vanilla
2-1/2 cups all purpose flour
1 teaspoon baking soda
1 teaspoon cream of tartar
granulated sugar

Mix powdered sugar, butter, egg & vanilla until creamy. Gradually add baking soda & cream of tartar to flour. Mix a little. Gradually add flour mixture to creamy mixture, blending well. When all mixed, cover and refrigerate for at least 2 hours. Divide dough into halves, roll each half 3/16th of an inch thick. On a lightly floured cloth covered board, cut into desired shapes with cookie cutters.

Sprinkle with granulated sugar. Lightly grease or line cookie sheet with parchment paper. Bake until edges are light brown, 7 to 8 minutes. Let cool and frost if desired. Makes about 5 dozen 2" cookies.